BEN THE INVENTOR

ROBIN STEVENSON
Illustrated by DAVID PARKINS

D0557157

ORCA BOOK PUBLISHERS

To Kai, whose creativity and energy inspire me

Library and Archives Canada Cataloguing in Publication

Stevenson, Robin, 1968-
Ben the inventor / Robin Stevenson.
(Orca echoes)

Issued also in electronic format.
ISBN 978-1-55469-802-8

I. Title. II. Series: Orca echoes
PS8637.T487B44 2011   JC813'.6   C2011-903473-5

First published in the United States, 2011
Library of Congress Control Number: 2011929244

Summary: Ben and his friend Jack try to use their inventions to stop the sale of Jack's house.

Orca Book Publishers gratefully acknowledges the support for its publishing programs
provided by the following agencies: the Government of Canada through the Canada Book
Fund and the Canada Council for the Arts, and the Province of British Columbia
through the BC Arts Council and the Book Publishing Tax Credit.

MIX
Paper from
responsible sources
FSC® C016245

*Orca Book Publishers is dedicated to preserving the environment and has printed this book
on paper certified by the Forest Stewardship Council®.*

Cover artwork and interior illustrations by David Parkins

ORCA BOOK PUBLISHERS   ORCA BOOK PUBLISHERS
PO Box 5626, Stn. B   PO Box 468
Victoria, BC Canada   Custer, WA USA
v8R 6s4   98240-0468

www.orcabook.com
Printed and bound in Canada.

14 13 12 11 • 4 3 2 1

Chapter One

Right in front of Ben's house was a speed bump. It led from Ben's front gate across the road to his friend Jack's front gate. Ben and Jack were best friends. It was summer holidays, so every day after breakfast, Jack walked along the top of the speed bump to Ben's house.

Today, something was different. Ben knew it as soon as he saw Jack's face. "What's wrong?" he asked.

Without a word, Jack turned and pointed back across the street. Ben looked, but he didn't see anything at first. Just Jack's wooden fence, the front gate and Jack's cat, Lulu, sitting in a patch of sunlight and licking her hind leg.

And then he saw the sign. A big, square, red and white sign with two words on it: *FOR SALE.*

"I don't get it," Ben said. An awful, cold feeling crept into his tummy. "You can't sell your house. Where would you live?"

"My mom got a new job," Jack said. "In Vancouver."

"Vancouver!" Ben stared at him.

"So we have to move."

"Move!"

Jack shrugged. "That's what she says."

"Tell her you won't go," Ben said.

"I already tried that," Jack said. "Last night."

"And?"

Jack shook his shaggy brown hair out of his eyes. "She said it was one of those things I didn't have a choice about."

Ben's mother said he didn't have a choice about a lot of things, such as brushing his teeth twice a day and sharing toys with his little sister, Stella. She also said it about going to school, instead of homeschooling like

3

Jack did, and turning off the computer after twenty minutes of *Alien Armada*. Still, moving to Vancouver was a very big thing not to have a choice about.

"That stinks," Ben said loudly. "It takes half a day to get to Vancouver. You have to go on the ferry and everything."

"I know."

"We won't be able to do stuff together anymore." Ben felt like he might cry. He scuffed the toe of his shoe on the sidewalk. "It's not fair."

Jack nodded. "That's what I said."

They stared at the sign. Neither of them spoke. Finally Ben said, "Well, I guess we'd better get to work."

Jack nodded. "We have inventions to invent."

"Because we're inventors. And inventors invent inventions," Ben said. He and Jack liked to say this because they liked using the word *invent* three times in one sentence. *Inventors invent inventions, inventors invent inventions.* Sometimes they said it over and over again until they laughed so hard they fell down in the grass.

But today, as they walked to their workshop in Ben's backyard, neither of them felt much like laughing.

Chapter Two

Ben's workshop was in the back corner of his yard. It used to be a garden shed, but now it was all his. It was filled with his stuff—a mountain of treasures he and Jack had collected. There were tin cans and pieces of pipe. There were hubcaps and old license plates. There were empty milk cartons, bits of wire, rusty hinges, broken TV remote controls, pieces of wood, glass jars and a hundred other things.

It is amazing, Ben thought, *how much good stuff people throw out*. He knew something most grown-ups didn't know: Junk plus Imagination equaled Great Inventions. The Great Invention he and Jack were working on at the moment was a catapult. Ben dragged an old shovel out of the shed.

"Yeah!" Jack said. He grabbed a brick. "Let's use this."

Ben laid the shovel on the ground. Jack slid the brick under the middle of the shovel's handle.

Ben pushed the blade down with his foot. The other end went up, like a teeter-totter. "Cool. Let's try it."

"We need something to launch," Jack said.

Ben looked around. "How about this?" He lifted up a large stone they had painted red and black like a ladybug.

"Fire-bellied toads!" Jack grinned. "That's perfect."

Ben dropped the stone into the shovel's blade. The blade slammed into the ground, and the other end of the shovel bounced up. "Okay. Try it."

Jack stepped on the raised end of the shovel. The blade shot up, sending the stone flying in a graceful arc. It sailed over his head and across the lawn.

"Cool." Ben thought for a moment. "If we put a bigger brick under the middle, the catapult would have more power."

"Yeah!" Jack dashed into the shed. When he came back, he was struggling with a large concrete block. "Oof! That's heavy."

The block thudded to the ground. Ben moved his foot just in time. He placed the catapult on top of the block.

"My turn," he said.

Jack put the ladybug stone back on the blade. "This is definitely a Stupendous Contraption," he said.

Stupendous Contraption was another one of the things they liked to say. They also said *fire-bellied toads*, which meant *absolutely perfect*. Ben couldn't even remember how most of their sayings had started, but they made him laugh.

Only not today, because all of it was going to end. The laughing, the inventing, the long summer days stuffed full of fun games. *It just isn't* right *that*

Jack's house is for sale, Ben thought. *It isn't fair.* With all his might, he jumped two-footed onto the shovel's handle. The ladybug stone rocketed into the air, higher and higher. It zoomed across the yard and crashed through the kitchen window of Ben's house.

Chapter Three

"What were you *thinking*?" Ben's mom asked him after she sent Jack home.

Ben hated it when people asked that question. He never knew how to answer it. Plus his mom had yelled at them, and she almost never did that. "I didn't know this would happen," he said. He was trying hard not to cry.

"Well, you aimed a large stone at a window. What did you think would happen?" She pointed at the broken glass scattered across the kitchen floor. Behind her, two-year-old Stella clung to her leg. "It's lucky no one was standing there, Ben. What if Stella had been in the kitchen?"

"It wasn't my fault!" Ben shouted. Then he burst into tears. He hated everything about today.

His mom put her hand on his head. "I know you didn't mean to break the window. But try to think before you do things, okay?"

Now that he had started crying, he couldn't seem to stop.

"Oh, Ben. I'm sorry I yelled at you and Jack. I was scared. Someone could have been hurt." She dropped to her knees, trying to look him in the eyes. "Ben?"

"Jack's moving," Ben said. "His house is for sale."

His mother looked startled. "Really? Are you sure?"

Ben grabbed his mom's arm and tugged her toward the living-room window. She picked Stella up and followed him. Ben pointed at the sign in front of Jack's house. "See? FOR SALE."

"Oh no." His mom sat down on the couch and pulled Stella onto her lap. She patted the cushion beside her. "I didn't know. I'm so sorry, Ben. Do you know where they're moving to?"

"His mom got a job in Vancouver." Ben rubbed his fists on his eyes, hard, until he saw little red stars. "I *hate* his mom."

"Ben!"

"Well, it isn't fair! How come kids don't get to choose anything?"

"You're angry and upset right now," his mom said. "I'm sorry Jack's moving. But sometimes people have to do things they don't want to do."

"He's my best friend," Ben said.

"What about Jessy?"

"She goes to camp all summer."

Ben's mom sighed. "Well, hopefully Jack's house won't sell too quickly."

"If it doesn't sell, does that mean they won't be able to move?" Ben asked.

"They probably can't buy a house in Vancouver until they sell this one," she said.

"I hope it never sells."

"I'm sure it will," she said. "It would be nice if they were here for the rest of the summer though. Until Jessy gets back from camp."

His mom didn't understand. Jessy was great, but she didn't know about *inventors invent inventions* or any of the other secret games he and Jack played. "Jessy can't take Jack's place," Ben said. "She's my school friend, and he's my holiday friend. Two different things." He frowned, trying to think of a way to make her understand. "Like you have Stella now, but you still want me."

She laughed. "You are right. Jack's special. But Vancouver isn't that far away. We can visit. It will be okay."

Maybe it will, Ben thought. Because his mom had given him an idea.

Ben was going to invent a Stupendous Plan.

Chapter Four

The next morning, Ben followed the speed bump to Jack's house. He knocked on the door. Jack's mom opened it. "Hi, Ben. Looking for Jack?"

Ben didn't answer. He didn't even say hello. "What if no one buys your house?" he asked instead.

"Someone had better buy it," she said, laughing. "We need the money to buy a new one."

So it was just as his mom had said. That was good. "Can Jack come out and play?" he asked.

"Sure." She turned and called up the stairs. "Jack! Ben's here."

Thump, thump, thump. Jack came down two steps at a time, still in his pajamas. "Hey! Let's go."

"Clothes," said his mom.

Jack looked down at his T. rex shirt and shorts. "Do I have to?"

"Yes, hurry up." She shooed him back upstairs. "Ben, I'll send him over as soon as he's had breakfast, okay?"

Ben nodded. Jack's mom sure would be surprised if she knew what he was planning.

By the time Jack arrived, Ben had already begun work.

"What are you building?" Jack asked.

"Another catapult," Ben said. "Sort of."

Jack looked worried. "Do you think that's a good idea?"

"It's a great idea," Ben said. "Listen. You don't want to move, right?"

Jack sat down on the grass and crisscrossed his legs. "Right."

"And if no one buys your house, you won't have to."

17

"Someone is coming to look at it tomorrow," Jack said. "They'll probably buy it."

"Not if we do something to stop them," Ben said.

"Like what?" Jack picked a blade of grass and chewed on it.

"Inventors invent inventions," Ben said, "and we need to make our most *Stupendous* Contraption ever."

For the rest of the day, under the hot summer sun, the two inventors worked the hardest they had ever worked. They only stopped twice, once for popsicles and once for cookies. They didn't even go inside to use the washroom. They just peed right in the vegetable garden. They aimed for the Swiss chard, since neither of them liked eating it anyway.

By the time their parents called them for dinner, the contraption was almost complete.

"Well?" Ben said. "What do you think?"

He and Jack stared at their invention. It began with a series of pipes and ended with a catapult. A new and improved catapult. It was twice as large and three times as powerful as the one Ben's mom had taken away. This one was the Ultimate Catapult. It was made of metal pipes and wood ramps and three different kinds of balls. It had a small solar panel and a race-car launcher with double-A batteries. It even had a toilet seat and some other stuff.

The solar panel didn't actually work, but it looked good. Really good.

"We should trademark this," Ben said. "So no one can copy it. It could be the Stupendous Contraption, TM."

"It really is stupendous," Jack whispered.

"I know." Ben felt like whispering too. He couldn't believe they had made something so amazing. It looked like a machine from one of his old Dr. Seuss books. "Should we test it?"

"Probably."

"Ben!" His mom was standing on the back deck. "Jack's mom wants him home, and our dinner's ready."

"Just a minute," Ben called back. "We have to finish something."

"That's what you said ten minutes ago," his mom said. "No more minutes, boys. You can play together again tomorrow."

Play, Ben thought. Someone was coming to look at Jack's house tomorrow! As if they had time to *play*.

Chapter Five

"Mom, do we have any balloons?" Ben asked.

His mom was stirring oatmeal on the stove. "I don't think so."

"Don't we have some left from Stella's birthday?" Ben looked at Stella, who was stacking cans of beans into a tower. "Stella, do you have balloons?"

"Balloons," Stella said happily. She knocked over her tower, and the cans tumbled to the floor with a crash. "Red balloons."

"Where are they, Stella?"

Stella's lower lip was sticking out like a fat pink worm. That meant she was in a stubborn mood. "Stella's red balloons," she said firmly.

"I know, Stella. It's important, okay?" Ben knelt down beside her. "I'll get you more. I promise." He looked at his mom. "If Stella lets me use her balloons, you can buy her more, right?"

"She doesn't have any, Ben." His mom grabbed the saucepan as the oatmeal started to boil over.

"Stella, where are they? The balloons?" Ben looked at Stella. "Tell me, okay?"

"Balloons go sky," Stella said. "Up, up." She shook her head, and her blond hair floated like a fluffy cloud around her chubby face.

Ben groaned in frustration and rocked back on his heels.

"Why do you need them, Ben?" his mom asked.

"I just do." He looked out the window. The Stupendous Contraption was hidden behind his workshop. He and Jack needed something to launch, but stones were too dangerous. Water balloons would have been perfect.

24

There was a knock at the front door. "It's Jack," Ben said. "I'll get it." He ran and let Jack in. "No balloons," he said. "What time are the people coming to look at the house?"

"Ten o'clock," Jack said. "Plus there's going to be an open house at twelve. Mom's going out, but she said I can stay here, if it's okay with your mom."

"That's fine," Ben's mom said from behind him. "Why don't you two go outside and play. It's a gorgeous day."

"What are we going to launch?" Jack asked.

They were looking at the small mountain of junk they had hauled out of the workshop. It glittered in the sun. "It's all metal and stuff," Ben said. "Too hard. We have to make people not buy your house, but we don't want to hurt anyone." He glanced at the kitchen window, which now had thick plastic taped over it.

Jack clapped his hands together. "I've got it."

"What?"

"Weeds," Jack said.

Ben looked around his yard. Morning glory vines grew all along the fence, twisted and green. Dandelions spotted the lawn. And behind the compost bin was a huge pile of weeds his mom had pulled from the vegetable garden.

"Fire-bellied toads! That's so perfect," Ben said. "We will make it rain weeds at your house."

Chapter Six

The catapult part of the Stupendous Contraption was made of a long wooden board. A toilet seat was duct-taped near one end. Ben and Jack gathered an armful of weeds and placed the pile inside the toilet seat.

"Test run," Ben said. He picked up a golf ball and dropped it into a sloping metal pipe. He and Jack both crossed their fingers and held their breath. The ball dropped out the other end of the tube. It rolled down a ramp and knocked over a wooden post. The post landed on the first of a long row of empty CD cases. Down they went, like dominoes. *Bing, bing, bing.*

The last CD case set off a mini-catapult, flinging a Ping-Pong ball into the air.

At this point, the Stupendous Contraption needed a little help. The Ping-Pong ball wasn't heavy enough to push the race car into the race-car launcher. Ben gave it a little shove. *Whoosh!* The race car zoomed along the plastic track and dropped off the end. It nudged a perfectly balanced soccer ball, which fell onto the end of the Ultimate Catapult.

The weeds flew into the air.

They landed in a pile less than two feet away.

The boys stared at it in disgust. "Well, that's no use at all," Ben said.

"It was pretty cool though." Jack grinned. "Like when the race car knocked off the soccer ball. That was great. And the domino thing."

"Cool but not useful. They were supposed to fly across the street to your house." Ben heard a car door slam. He stood up and looked toward the street.

A blond woman in a suit was getting out of a car. "Is that her? The real estate person?"

"Must be."

They watched as a second car pulled up. A tall bald man got out. The real estate woman waved to him. Then they walked through Jack's front gate together.

Jack turned to Ben. "I guess that's the man who wants to buy my house."

Ben made a face. "No way."

"So what are we going to do?"

"Well, launching the weeds didn't work. So I guess we move on to Stupendous Plan B," Ben said.

"Okay. What's Stupendous Plan B?"

Ben didn't actually have a Plan B, let alone a *Stupendous* Plan B. He thought fast. "We'll just carry the weeds across to your yard," he said. "We'll spread them on the lawn while the real estate agent is inside showing that man your house."

A grin spread slowly across Jack's face. "And he will think the weeds are growing there!"

"Yeah, and he won't buy the house because there is too much gardening to do," Ben said.

"Perfect," Jack said, gathering up an armful of weeds. "Fire-bellied toads! Let's go."

Chapter Seven

Ben opened his back door and stuck his head inside. "Mom? We're just going for a walk, okay?"

"Stella, stop that." His mom grabbed Stella's arm. "Spit it out, honey." She popped her fingers into Stella's mouth and fished out something small and blue. "Lego, this time. She just puts everything in her mouth."

"We'll be back soon," Ben said.

"Okay. Stay on this block," his mom said.

"Oh, we will." Ben nudged Jack. "Come on."

Ben and Jack picked up the weeds they had piled by Ben's front gate. They carried them across the speed bump. Then, very quietly, they scattered them around Jack's lawn. Dandelions on the grass. Morning glory vine on the rose bushes. All kinds of dead green stuff along the path.

They were almost finished when the front door opened. "Run!" Jack whispered.

Ben followed Jack, dashing down the sidewalk. He thought he heard a woman yell after them, but he didn't stop. They ran to the end of their block and hid behind a tree. Then they both sank to the ground, giggling like crazy.

"Do you think they saw us?" Jack asked.

"Probably. It doesn't matter though. They don't know who we are." Ben stopped laughing. He frowned. "We should have put the weeds down before they arrived."

Jack laughed. "Yeah, they must think they are the fastest-growing weeds ever."

"Stupendous Weeds!" Ben said, cracking up.

"Stupendous Weeds!" Jack grabbed him by the shoulders and pinned him down, half hugging him

and half wrestling with him. After a minute, he let Ben go. He sat back on his heels and gave a long sigh. "I sure hope our plan works. 'Cause I really, really, really don't want to move."

Ben and Jack watched from a safe distance as the bald man drove away. Then they snuck up to Jack's house and peeked through the fence. The real estate agent was still there. She was picking up all the weeds and piling them in one corner of the yard. Ben thought it was funny to see someone gardening in a suit. But, from the look on her face, she didn't find it very amusing at all.

"Let's get out of here," he whispered. He and Jack dashed across the speed bump and into Ben's backyard.

Ben flopped down on the grass, laughing. "Whew. That was great."

Jack rolled on top of him and pinned him down again. He liked to wrestle. "Yeah," he said. "That was fun." Then he stopped smiling. He sat up and looked at his watch. "The open house is in one hour. The weeds will be cleaned up by then."

For a minute, Ben had forgotten they weren't just playing. "I know," he said. "We need another plan. Plan C."

It was lucky he and Jack were good at coming up with plans. Inventors were smart like that.

Chapter Eight

"Okay," Ben said. "What kind of things would make someone not buy a house?"

"Um, if it was falling down or something like that?" Jack said.

Ben shook his head. "We can't make your house fall down. Anyway, even if we had dynamite or something, it would be a bad idea. You still have to live in it."

"I didn't mean we should really make it fall down. I meant, we could make people think it was falling down."

"Hmm." Ben thought about that. "How?"

Jack stood up. "We go to the open house."

"Can we? Are kids allowed?"

"My mom told me anyone could go," Jack said. "She thinks all the nosy people in the neighborhood will be there." He frowned. "She's been cleaning like mad. She even made me take down my *Star Wars* posters and hide them under my bed."

"Wow." Jack's bedroom walls had always been covered with *Star Wars* posters. Ben couldn't even picture it without them. It made him think about how awful it would be if Jack moved. Someone else might get his room and make it look completely different.

There was no way he could let that happen. "Okay," he said. "We'll go to the open house." Then he had a great idea. "In disguise!"

"Fire-bellied toads!" Jack said.

Ben and Jack dragged the costume trunk out from under his bed. It was filled with all kinds of stuff.

There was a robot costume from when Ben had loved robots more than anything. There were the Viking costumes he and Jessy had made together. His old Halloween costumes were in there too. There was a skeleton costume, a devil costume and even a shark costume.

But there was nothing that seemed quite right for an open house.

Jack tried on a fake mustache. "What do you think?"

"Goofy." Ben put on a construction hat. "How about this?"

"We're not going to look like grown-ups," Jack said glumly. "We're too short."

That gave Ben an idea—a Stupendous Idea. "Jack! I know. I can sit on your shoulders. We can pretend we're one person."

Jack's face lit up. "Cool." He pulled a long black cloak out of the trunk. "This will hide me. All that will show is your head."

By twelve o'clock, Ben and Jack were ready to go. Ben stood on the deck steps. Jack bent down. Ben scrambled onto his shoulders. The cloak was tied around his neck. It hung down below Jack's knees. All that showed was Ben's head at the top, and Jack's running shoes at the bottom.

Ben had drawn on a mustache with his mom's eyeliner. He had the construction hat on. It was time to put Plan C into action.

Chapter Nine

"Hurry up," Ben said. It felt odd sitting on Jack's shoulders. Wobbly.

"You're heavy!" Jack said. He was walking carefully across the speed bump. "And I can't see where I'm going."

"Keep going straight," Ben said. "Now stop. Step up on the sidewalk."

"Are you sure this is a good idea?" Jack asked.

Ben was not sure. He didn't have any better ideas though. "It will be fine," he said. "Keep going. You're on the front path. Almost at your front door." He could see people walking around inside. Mostly strangers, but there was the woman from two doors down, and the man who lived in the corner house.

Jack's mom had been right about the neighbors coming to look.

"Are there lots of people?" Jack asked.

"Can't you hear them?"

"Yeah." Jack stopped at the front door. "Should I just walk in?"

Ben nodded. Then he remembered Jack couldn't see him. "Yes," he said. "Straight ahead. Then a couple of steps left. Yes, perfect."

"Now what?" Jack whispered.

"Stop talking," Ben said. "You are the body, remember? I am the head." His heart was racing. The real estate agent was across the room. She was looking right at him. Ben looked away quickly.

A man with a beard was walking toward the front door. Ben waited until the man was a few feet away. "Ahem," he said.

The man looked up at him.

"This house is falling apart," Ben said. He tried to make his voice low, like a grown man.

"There is a rat living in the roof. And, um, it leaks when it rains."

"The rat leaks?" The man hid a grin behind his hand.

Ben shook his head. "The *roof* leaks. And a new roof costs thousands of dollars."

"It does indeed." The man waved over a woman who was admiring the stained glass window in the living room.

She smiled and crossed the room. "Yes?" She looked at Ben and laughed. "Well, hello."

Ben noticed that she was very pregnant. "Hello," he said.

"Darling, this gentleman was telling me the house needs a new roof." The man put an arm around her waist.

"Is that right?" She shook her head. "I'm sorry to hear that. A new roof costs a lot of money."

"Exactly," Ben said. "So you don't really want to buy this house."

The real estate agent appeared behind them. She grabbed Ben's cloak and yanked it off. "You two again!"

Ben jumped off Jack's shoulders and stood beside him. He was so scared, he could hardly breathe.

"Off you go," the real estate agent said. "Go on. Out!"

"Oh, it's okay." The pregnant woman was laughing. "They're just having fun."

"Well, their fun cost me a sale." The real estate agent glared at them. "The man who looked at the house this morning said he didn't want to live across the street from a couple of badly behaved kids."

Good, Ben thought. He didn't want to live across the street from a grumpy bald man.

Chapter Ten

"Success!" Ben said once they were back in his yard. "It worked! No grumpy bald man!"

Jack looked less sure. "She was pretty mad," he said. "I hope she doesn't tell my parents."

"Me too." Ben didn't think his mom would be too happy about Plan B or Plan C. He looked across the street, and his heart sank. People were streaming through Jack's gate. Lots of them. Old people. Families. Young couples. Even a woman with a yappy dog tucked under her arm.

Jack watched them too. "This stinks," he said. He dropped the cape and sat down on the grass. "I feel like it's not even my house anymore."

"This really stinks," Ben said. There was a big lump in his throat. His eyes stung with tears. He had a feeling all the plans in the world might not be enough to make Jack's family stay.

The next day, Ben's mom made his favorite food for dinner: pizza with pineapple and pepperoni, no sauce and not too much cheese.

"Ben," his mom said. "There's something I have to tell you."

Ben put down his slice of pizza and looked at her. He had a bad feeling.

"Jack's mom called." She looked at him. Her eyes looked sad, and there were frown lines in between them.

Ben wondered if he was in trouble. Maybe the real estate agent had told Jack's parents about what they had done. He hoped that was it. Because being in trouble for Plan B and Plan C would be better than the other thing Jack's mom might call about.

"They have an offer on their house, Ben. A good offer." His mom made a face. "I'm so sorry. They're moving. But they won't go for another month. At least Jack will be here until the end of the summer."

"It's not fair," Ben said. He squeezed his eyes tight, trying not to cry. One hot tear snuck out. "He's my best friend."

"I know. You will miss him. And he will miss you." His mom stood up. She walked over to him and gave him a long hard hug. "We will visit. I promise. And he can come here too. His mom says he can even come and stay with us for a weekend once they have settled in. Thanksgiving, maybe."

"It won't be the same," Ben said.

"You're right. It won't be the same." His mom sighed. "That's life, Ben. Things change."

Maybe so, Ben thought, *but I don't have to like it.*

August went by too fast. It was warm and sunny. Ben and Jack spent almost every day together. They played with water guns. They picked blackberries and ate them right off the prickly green vines. They played soccer and hit golf balls against the fence. They pretended to explore other planets. But mostly they invented things. Because they were inventors.

"And inventors invent inventions," Jack said. He was lying on Ben's deck, writing the alphabet on a large piece of paper. Blocky capital letters stretched in neat single file across the page.

"That's right." Ben was working on his own alphabet page, slowly writing each letter with a fine-tipped black marker. His writing was not as tidy as Jack's. Ben liked to write fast more than he liked to write carefully. But today he wanted his letters

53

to be perfect, because this might be their most important invention ever. *X, Y, Z*, Ben wrote. "There," he said. "I'm done. Ready?"

"Ready." Jack slid his paper above Ben's so the two alphabets lined up. *A* under *A*, *B* under *B*, *C* under *C*.

"What code, do you think?" Ben asked. "Maybe a Plus Three Shift?" His mom had given him a great new book about how to write and read secret codes.

"Plus Two," Jack said. "Two like you and me. Because we will always be friends. Even if we don't live close to each other."

"Fire-bellied toads," Ben said. "Plus Two then." He grinned and slid his page along two letters. Now the letters lined up with *C* under *A*, *D* under *B*, *E* under *C*, and so on. Then he taped the two sheets together. "This can be yours," he said. "And we'll make another one for me."

"Fire-bellied toads," Jack said. "I'll email every week."

"Me too." Ben looked at the decoder and grinned. "And no one else will be able to read our messages."

Chapter Eleven

At the end of August, Jack's family packed all their things into a giant moving truck. Their house looked very strange with nothing in it.

"Bigger," Ben said. "It looks way bigger now."

They were standing in Jack's empty bedroom. Jack's mom had told them it was time to say goodbye. "We don't really have to though," Jack said. "Because we can email each other tonight, if we want to."

"Plus we can visit each other," Ben said. "My mom says you can even stay with us if you want. For a weekend."

Jack tackled him and pulled him down to the bare wood floor. "Yes! And we'll do something Stupendous."

Ben nodded. "We sure will," he said. He knew they would always be friends. But he still felt sad. He had really loved having a friend right across the street.

A week later, Ben sent Jack an email. It read:

Hi Jack!!! You'll never guess who bought your house. Remember the pregnant woman and the man with the beard who were at the open house? Well, they just moved in. I guess they didn't believe us about the roof. They have a little baby now. It cries all the time. Loudly! But here's the good part. They also have a kid who is eight! A girl called Sarah. You can meet her when you come and visit. And guess what else? She put Star Wars posters all over your room. She is nice, but I wish you still lived there. I miss you. From your friend, Ben the Inventor.

Ben stopped typing. That was long enough. It took a long time, writing messages in code. He had to write his emails the normal way first. Then he had to put them in Plus Two Shift code. His mom was even letting him have extra computer time to do it. Just typing *Hi Jack!!!* took him a couple of minutes. It became *Jk Lcem!!!* Ben loved that. *Jk Lcem!!!*

Finally, Ben had his message all in code. *Ben the Inventor* became *Dgp vjg Kpxgpvqt*. It looked Stupendous. He grinned. It was going to take Jack hours to decode the whole email.

Ben yawned and stretched. Through the window, he could see Sarah. She was wearing 3-D glasses and making crazy designs with chalk on the sidewalk in front of her house. Her hair was tangled and long, and she had bare feet. He had played with her a couple of times already. She even wanted to walk to school with him and Jessy when school started next week.

When Ben thought about it, Plan B and C hadn't been a total failure. Sarah's parents had liked that there were other kids living on the street. They had even liked the way he and Jack had dressed up at the open house. So it was thanks to Plan B and C that Sarah lived across the street instead of the grumpy bald man.

Outside, Sarah stood up. She put down her chalk, and she walked across the speed bump.

Quickly, Ben pressed *SEND*. Then he closed the laptop.

Sarah was about to knock on the door, and Ben had promised to show her his workshop.

Robin Stevenson is the author of many novels for children and teens. *Ben the Inventor* is Robin's second Orca Echo about Ben, and both stories were inspired by her own son. Robin lives, writes and teaches in Victoria, British Columbia.